The Storekeeper

a stageplay in three acts

David R. Beshears

Greybeard Publishing
Washington State

ISBN 978-0-9891764-9-1

The stage play may not be performed without the permission of Greybeard Publishing.

Please contact Greybeard Publishing for performance fee prices.

High schools and some nonprofit organizations may be able to perform The Storekeeper free of charge. Please contact us to request a release.

Greybeard Publishing
P.O. Box 480
McCleary, WA 98557

Author Page: www.davidrbeshears.com
Publisher Site: www.greybeardpublishing.com

WGA #1612261

The Storekeeper

Cast of Characters

THE STOREKEEPER, *the man behind whatever is going on.*
Middle-aged, friendly, outgoing but not giving anything away.
Casual clothes; flannel shirt with sleeves rolled up.

WILL DAWSON, *quiet, confident loner.*
Mid-30s. Wears black jeans, light windbreaker. Appears
comfortable being on his own. He has a thoughtful manner and
doesn't let the unexpected surprise him.

PETER HARRIS,
HELEN HARRIS, *young couple.*
Both in their 20s. He dresses in light slacks and a short-sleeved
button shirt. She dresses in summer shorts and a pullover
blouse. They appear as deer-in-headlights in their current
situation.

MOLLY CHANDLER, *teenager with secrets.*
About 16 years old, wears faded jeans and light jacket. Has a
knit cap on her head, what hair is showing could use a
brushing. She's withdrawn, on edge, as if she may jump at the
next loud noise. She's been through some trauma.

MRS. MAYFIELD, *elderly black woman.*
Hair more gray than black, pulled back and bound in a bun.
She's carrying a few extra pounds, wears a clean but well-worn
dress, and clutches at a black plastic purse. She's kind but
defensive.

WAYNE SAUNDERS, *disgruntled.*
About 30, dresses in loose slacks and sport jacket. Disgruntled
with a world that just won't give him a break.

EDIE PAULSEN, *woman with a bit of a past.*
About 30, but she looks worn out, as if life has beaten her
down. Her clothes may have been nice at one time, but now look
as worn out and used as their owner. Her makeup is too much
and yet not enough. She's a good person who's been around the
block too many times.

Stage play Structure
Three acts, each with a different set. Each act has 2 scenes; no set change between scenes.

Setting
A general store, old and all worn out, sits alone on a long-forgotten highway.

The Sets

ACT 1 : Front of Store
A wooden porch runs the width of the weathered storefront. On the porch is a wooden bench and an old, rickety rocking chair.

A faded sign above the store reads "General Store". A sign on the wall next to the front screen door reads "Lunch Counter". At the corner of the building is a small sign with an arrow pointing behind the store that reads "To Trains".

Optional: To one side of the store is a very old gas pump with an equally old sign on it that reads "No Gas".

ACT 2 : General Store Interior
There is a small checkout counter with cash register near the screen door that leads outside.

The lunch counter is long enough to accommodate two tall stools. On the wall behind it a sign reads "Sandwiches". Nearby are two small tables, each with three chairs. To one side stands a single, six-foot long row of store shelves filled with boxed and canned goods.

A small sign with an arrow pointing to a hallway leading off-stage reads "To Trains".

ACT 3 : Train Station Interior

There is a single ticket window behind a counter. A sign beside the ticket window reads:"Southbound 8:00 AM".

There is a long, worn, wooden bench for passenger waiting.

A sign over an opening at stage rear reads "Gate 1". Hanging on the wall beside the opening is the small sign with an arrow pointing to the opening that reads "To Trains".

ACT 1

SCENE 1.

AT RISE: The front of the store. The porch.
MRS. MAYFIELD sits primly in the rocking
chair, gently rocking. She clutches a black,
plastic purse in her lap.

STOREKEEPER sits on the bench next to the
rocking chair. He's relaxed, has one arm
draped along the back of the bench.

The screen door opens and WAYNE
SAUNDERS steps out onto the porch. He has
a bottle of cola in hand. Hinges screech noisily
as the screen door closes behind him.

> WAYNE
> I put a pair of quarters on the
> counter.
>> (He doesn't sound all that
>> pleased about it)

> STOREKEEPER
> I thank you, Mr. Saunders.

> WAYNE
> Yeah. Whatever.

He takes a long pull on his cola, sighs tiredly
and looks out at the highway.

> WAYNE (CONT'D)
> Ya' get many cars come by
> here?

> STOREKEEPER
> Not a one.

                    WAYNE
          Doesn't that make it tough to
          earn a livin'? Ya gotta have
          customers to run a store,
          don't ya?

The Storekeeper gives a slow nod. He wears a
knowing, confident smile.

                    STOREKEEPER
          You are here, Mr. Saunders.
          And you have made a
          purchase. That would make
          you a customer.

                    WAYNE
               (Holds the bottle up in
               salute)
          Glad to help, Storekeeper.

He takes another swallow of his cola. He looks
then to Mrs. Mayfield.

                    WAYNE (CONT'D)
          So what's your story, lady?

                    MRS. MAYFIELD
          I beg your pardon?

                    WAYNE
          What brings you here?
               (hint of sarcasm)
          You a customer, too?

                    MRS. MAYFIELD
               (defenses going up)
          I'm sorry, sir. I don't believe—

STOREKEEPER
Oh, dear. Where are my
manners? Mrs. Mayfield, allow
me to introduce Mr. Wayne
Saunders.   Mr. Saunders, this
wonderful lady is Mrs.
Mayfield.

WAYNE
Mrs. Mayfield.

MRS. MAYFIELD
(composed)
Mr. Saunders.

STOREKEEPER
Mrs. Mayfield is on her way to
visit her sister. Isn't that
right, Mrs. Mayfield?

MRS. MAYFIELD
That's right. Cecilia asked if I
might stay with her for a
spell. She's all alone, now that
her husband Walter passed
away.

She eyes Wayne. She continues to maintain
distance, but certainly doesn't want to appear
rude.

MRS. MAYFIELD (CONT'D)
And you, Mr. Saunders?

WAYNE
(shrugs)
Leavin' one city, headin' for
another.

MRS. MAYFIELD
I see.

She thinks on that. Her rocking slows to an
easy stop. She pauses, begins rocking again,
slow and steady.

        MRS. MAYFIELD (CONT'D)
    That sounds sad.

        STOREKEEPER
    I'm sure Mr. Saunders is
    simply seeking out new and
    exciting opportunities. Isn't
    that right, Wayne?

        WAYNE
    Exactly. I'm not one to sit
    still. Heck no. Ya' gotta reach
    out and take life by the scruff
    a' the neck.

        STOREKEEPER
    Of course.

        WAYNE
    The system works against
    folks like me. The breaks are
    never gonna go my way all on
    their own.
       (sharp, sure nod)
    So I gotta work that much
    harder'n everybody else.

        STOREKEEPER
       (supportive)
    Make your own breaks, so to
    speak.

        WAYNE
    Exactly.

> MRS. MAYFIELD
> (attempting to sound
> genuine)
> Good for you, Mr. Saunders.

She is now finished with this particular conversation, having met whatever etiquette requirements may have been due here. She returns her focus to her rocking.

> WAYNE
> Yeah, well...

Wayne finishes his cola. He looks around for where to dispose of the bottle.

The Storekeeper motions to the screen door.

> STOREKEEPER
> The recycle bin is inside, sir,
> next to the pop cooler.

Hint of annoyance from Wayne at having to take the empty back into the store and return it to right near where he got it to begin with.

He nonetheless goes to the screen door, opens it and goes inside.

> MRS. MAYFIELD
> That young man does have
> issues.

> STOREKEEPER
> Yes he does, Mrs. Mayfield.
> Yes he does.

A few moments later he looks offstage, smiles.

> STOREKEEPER (CONT'D)
> Ah. The Harris couple.

PETER HARRIS and HELEN HARRIS walk
onto the stage.

Mrs. Mayfield stops her rocking yet again. She
leans forward just a might and looks in the
direction of the newcomers.

> MRS. MAYFIELD
> You know them?

> STOREKEEPER
> Oh, but of course.

Peter and Helen approach the porch steps.

Storekeeper gives a pleasant, welcoming nod
and smile from his seated position on the
bench.

> STOREKEEPER (CONT'D)
> Hello, dear friends.

Both Peter and Helen appear disoriented,
bewildered. This is reflected in their lost gaze
and muffled speech.

> HELEN
> Hello.

> PETER
> Yes. Yes, hello.
> (looks offstage)
> I... our car broke down.

> STOREKEEPER
> Of course it did. Of course it
> did.

> PETER
> Out on... out on the uh...
> highway.

Helen clutches her husband's arm.

> HELEN
> We've been walking...
> (the statement fades away)

> MRS. MAYFIELD
> You poor dear.

> HELEN
> A long time.

Helen looks now in the direction from which they came. She looks to Peter, and then up at Storekeeper and Mrs. Mayfield.

> HELEN (CONT'D)
> Our car.

> PETER
> That's right. Our car. It broke down.

> STOREKEEPER
> Why don't you go inside and get freshened up? It's a warm morning. And it's going to get warmer.

> PETER
> (beat)
> Yeah. Sounds good...

Peter and Helen take the steps up onto the porch. As they approach the screen door, Helen smiles meekly at Storekeeper.

> HELEN
> Yes. Thank you... so much.

STOREKEEPER
My pleasure, Helen.

Helen looks taken aback at hearing the
Storekeeper speak her name.

HELEN
Excuse me... but I--

Peter opens the screen door, gently takes
Helen by the elbow.

PETER
(drawing Helen inside)
Come on, Helen.

They go into the store. The screen door noisily
clatters closed.

Mrs. Mayfield leans back in the chair and
returns to her slow, comfortable rocking.

MRS. MAYFIELD
Such like a nice couple. You
say you know them?

STOREKEEPER
But of course, Mrs. Mayfield.
Helen and Peter.
(beat)
Yes. A nice couple. Very nice.

MRS. MAYFIELD
They seem to be a bit...
turned around.

STOREKEEPER
The long walk, no doubt.

MRS. MAYFIELD
Yes, I'm sure you're right.

She leans forward and looks offstage in the direction from which the Harris couple arrived a few moments earlier.

> MRS. MAYFIELD (CONT'D)
> My, my. More company, looks like.

> STOREKEEPER
> (looking offstage)
> Ah! Looks to be the young Molly Chandler!

MOLLY CHANDLER comes onstage wearing a light, well-worn backpack. She comes up to the foot of the steps, lets the backpack slide down until she can set it at her feet.

> STOREKEEPER (CONT'D)
> Good morning to you, Molly.

Molly doesn't seem to catch the fact that Storekeeper knows her name.

> MOLLY
> You the Storekeeper here?

> STOREKEEPER
> That would be me. And how are you this fine day?

> MOLLY
> I could use some water.

> STOREKEEPER
> You'll find the drinking fountain inside. Near the restrooms.

> MOLLY
> Thanks.

Molly picks her backpack up by a shoulder
strap, climbs the steps up onto the porch. She
starts toward the screen door.

> MOLLY (CONT'D)
> I've been on the road for--

Molly hesitates, as if she knew something, or
thought she knew something, and now it's
gone.

> MOLLY (CONT'D)
> I've been walking...
> (confusion)
> ... been out... all morning...

> STOREKEEPER
> The water inside is cool and
> refreshing.

> MOLLY
> Yeah. Thanks.

Molly opens the screen door and goes inside,
hinges screeching, door clapping shut behind
her.

> MRS. MAYFIELD
> You recognized that poor girl.
> Molly, you said.

> STOREKEEPER
> Molly Chandler. Difficult time
> at home, I'm afraid. She's
> been on her own now for...
> well, for some time.

> MRS. MAYFIELD
> (confusion of her own)
> But... she didn't seem to know
> you.

STOREKEEPER
(very matter-of-fact)
No, of course not. Why would
she?

MRS. MAYFIELD
But... I don't understand.
(beat)
And the couple... they didn't
know you either.

The screen door opens and Wayne steps
outside. He looks curiously back inside, eases
the screen door closed.

WAYNE
Hey, Storekeeper. You may
not get any cars passing by
here, but you sure get a lot of
foot traffic.

STOREKEEPER
It does look to be the day for
it, doesn't it?

WAYNE
Kinda' odd, don't you think?
Way out here, middle of
nowhere, folks just walkin' up
to your store?

STOREKEEPER
Why would you think it odd,
Wayne?

Wayne is surprised by the question, quickly
recovers.

WAYNE
Cuz, you know... you're out
here, *in the middle of
nowhere*?

STOREKEEPER
Nowhere, sir? I like to think of
my little slice of paradise as
the center of the universe.

WAYNE
Really? You're kiddin', right?

STOREKEEPER
I have an amazing sense of
humor, Mr. Saunders, but
when it comes to my world, I
do not... *kid*.

WAYNE
All right, all right. No need to
get tetchy.

STOREKEEPER
(thin smile)
Not at all, Wayne. Not at all.

Mrs. Mayfield clutches more tightly at the
plastic purse in her lap, gives an amiable nod.

MRS. MAYFIELD
I find it very peaceful here.

WAYNE
No argument there, lady.
Quiet as a grave.

STOREKEEPER
(smirk)
'cept for all that foot traffic?

WAYNE
Yeah. 'cept for that.

MRS. MAYFIELD
It feels like it's gonna be a
warm one, though. Don't you
think?

STOREKEEPER
I expect that's true, Mrs.
Mayfield.
(looks offstage)
And this would be Will
Dawson.

WILL DAWSON saunters onto the stage, a tall
walking staff in hand.

WAYNE
More foot traffic. Cancel that
"quiet as a grave".

Will approaches the steps to the porch.

WILL
Hello, folks.

STOREKEEPER
Good morning to you, Will.

WILL
(wary)
Morning. Do I know you?

STOREKEEPER
I wouldn't think so.

WILL
Then--

> STOREKEEPER
> (cuts him off)
> Mrs. Mayfield, Mr. Saunders,
> may I present Will Dawson.
> An archeologist, if I'm not
> mistaken. Did I get that right?

> WILL
> You seem to be "not
> mistaken" about a number of
> things, Storekeeper.

> STOREKEEPER
> It comes with the job, my
> friend.

> WILL
> Uh, huh. Which would be?

> STOREKEEPER
> (indicates the surroundings)
> That would be minding the
> store, of course.

Mrs. Mayfield ceases her rocking, leans
forward, back straight, and enters the
conversation.

> MRS. MAYFIELD
> Good morning to you, Mr.
> Dawson.

> WILL
> (slight nod of the head)
> Mornin', ma'am. Please, call
> me Will.

> MRS. MAYFIELD
> Nice to meet you, Will.

Mrs. Mayfield shifts back again, and again returns to her slow, steady rocking, clutching her purse. Obligations met.

>   WILL
>   (acknowledges Wayne)
>   Mr. Saunders.

>   WAYNE
>   Will. Been walkin' long?

Will thinks on that a moment, looks curiously in the direction he traveled from, then looks back to Wayne.

>   WILL
>   Some. I suppose.

There comes the haunting SOUND of a TRAIN WHISTLE in the distance.

>   STOREKEEPER
>   Ah...

Storekeeper smiles contentedly, waits for the sound to fade.

>   STOREKEEPER (CONT'D)
>   Must be eight o'clock.

Will doubts that. He reaches into his pocket, pulls out an old pocket watch and looks at the time.

>   WILL
>   It's nine thirty.

>   STOREKEEPER
>   (patiently)
>   No... I'm pretty sure it's eight.

                    WILL
                (holding up his watch)
            Never more'n a minute off,
            Storekeeper.
                    (returns his watch to his
                    pocket)

                    STOREKEEPER
            I beg to differ, Will. It is eight
            o'clock. Here.
                    (knowing calm)
            Here, it is always eight
            o'clock.

                    WAYNE
            What's that supposed to
            mean?

                    STOREKEEPER
            Just what I said, Wayne. No
            more, no less.

Wayne appears annoyed, yet again. He sighs
and shakes his head, directs his words to Will.

                    WAYNE
            He always talks like that.

                    STOREKEEPER
            Do I?

                    WAYNE
            Yeah. You do.

As their exchange fades, Will uses the head of
his staff to indicate the "To Trains" sign
hanging on the wall.

                    WILL
            You have a train station back
            there, Storekeeper?

> STOREKEEPER
> Of a sort. Up to now, the
> train's never had cause to
> stop.

> WILL
> And it does now?

Storekeeper gets a warm feeling all over...

> STOREKEEPER
> Soon enough, my friend. It
> will soon enough.

END OF SCENE SEQUENCE:

The LIGHTS slowly begin to DIM, though it remains bright enough to see.

Mrs. Mayfield rises unhurriedly up from the rocking chair. With that, Storekeeper stands and walks to the screen door. He holds it open for her.

Mrs. Mayfield enters the store, still clutching her purse.

Storekeeper looks to Wayne, who decides to go inside, follows Mrs. Mayfield through the door.

Storekeeper closes the screen door, returns to his bench as Will climbs the steps up onto the porch.

Will takes a seat in the rocking chair, holds his staff casually in front of him.

They calmly and quietly take in the scene before them.

END OF SCENE:

SCENE 2.

LIGHTS slowly return to normal.

The Storekeeper and Will Dawson continue to look out at the landscape before them.

After a few moments, Will shifts uncomfortably in the chair, leans forward, both hands grasping his staff. He continues to look outward.

> WILL
> Storekeeper, I get the feeling
> that something isn't right. And
> furthermore, I'm pretty sure
> that whatever it is that's going
> on, you are at the heart of it.

Storekeeper leans back, rests his arm along the back of the bench.

> STOREKEEPER
> Things seem right enough to
> me, Will.

> WILL
> Now that's something right
> there. You knew my name
> when I got here. You know
> me. How is that?

> STOREKEEPER
> Why wouldn't I know you?

> WILL
> Because we've never met.
> Because I've never seen you
> before.

                    STOREKEEPER
          What does that have to do
          with it?

                        WILL
                    (frustration)
          <u>That</u>. What you just said. See,
          it makes sense. But it
          shouldn't make sense. None
          of this should make sense...
          none at all.

He grows intensely thoughtful. His words grow
soft.

                    WILL (CONT'D)
          There's stuff I should know. I
          <u>know</u> there's stuff I should
          know that I don't know. There
          are... *holes*... in my mind.
          Empty places. I feel it. I'm not
          all here. I'm not... *complete*.

                    STOREKEEPER
          Will Dawson, you are the most
          complete person here.

Will puts his weight on his staff and stands
up. He steps to the edge of the porch.

                        WILL
          Here. Just where is that?
          Where is... *here*?

                    STOREKEEPER
          "Here" is the center of the
          universe, my friend.

Will turns his head and looks back at the
Storekeeper.

              WILL
Your store. The center of the
universe. Where it is always
eight o'clock in the morning.

        STOREKEEPER
Exactly, Mr. Dawson.

Will shakes his head in frustration and again
looks out before them.

              WILL
Sorry... I can't put my finger
on it, but somehow that's
wrong. Or... it *should* be
wrong. That is wrong, where
we are is wrong, and all of
us... we are all so very, very
wrong.
    (sighs tiredly, despondently)
Wrong, wrong, wrong...

The Storekeeper's cool, calm and collected
sense of well being remains strong. He stands
and steps up beside Will.

        STOREKEEPER
Do not be overly concerned,
Will. All is well. Of all that you
may doubt the world around
you, I believe you know that
you can trust me.
    (gentle smile)
Is that not so?

                    WILL
What I believe is that you are
smack-dab in the middle of
what's going on. Trust you?
        (another shake of the head)
Let us say that I have some
concern when it comes to
your motives. I should
probably fear you. We all
should fear you.

                STOREKEEPER
And yet you do not fear me.

                    WILL
No. I don't.

                STOREKEEPER
That is good.
        (beat)
As for my motives, they are
brimming over with good
intentions.

                    WILL
We'll see.
        (sees someone approaching
        from off stage)
More company?

                STOREKEEPER
How nice. It's Edie.
        (satisfied)
And so. We are all here.

At that strange observation, Will gives
Storekeeper a curious look.

Before he can say anything, EDIE PAULSEN
comes on stage and approaches the foot of the
steps.

                    EDIE
                (numbly)
            Excuse me. I think I'm lost.

                STOREKEEPER
            Hello, Edie. No need to worry.
            You are exactly where you
            need to be.

Edie looks at the store, then at Will, then back
at the Storekeeper.

                    EDIE
            I am?

                STOREKEEPER
            You certainly are. Welcome,
            my dear.

Edie looks slowly over at Will.

Will gives her a friendly nod of the head.

                    WILL
            Will Dawson. And I am as
            confused as you are.

                    EDIE
            I seriously doubt that.

                STOREKEEPER
            Will Dawson, this is Edie
            Paulsen. Edie, meet Will
            Dawson.

                    EDIE
                (unenthusiastic)
            Hey.

                    WILL
            Nice to meet you.

Edie looks around her, behind her, back again to the two gentlemen on the porch.

>   EDIE
> If you say so.

She takes a step to one side, then another. She looks up at the sign reading "To Trains".

She looks pointedly then at Storekeeper.

>   EDIE (CONT'D)
> Are we dead?

This gets Will's attention, and he now also looks pointedly at Storekeeper.

Storekeeper looks genuinely surprised.

>   STOREKEEPER
> Oh, my. No. Absolutely not.
> What would make you think
> such a thing?

>   EDIE
>   (flat statements)
> I don't know how I got here. I
> don't know where here is. I
> don't know where I was
> before I was here.

>   WILL
> Come to think on it, neither
> do I.

>   STOREKEEPER
> Now you two stop all this
> foolishness. You are most
> definitely not dead. This isn't
> heaven. Or hell. Or anything
> of the sort.

> WILL
> The center of the universe?

> STOREKEEPER
> Exactly right. Yes. Exactly
> right.
>   (proud)
> Welcome. Welcome to the
> center of the universe.

Edie points to the "To Trains" sign.

> EDIE
> With train service...

> STOREKEEPER
> For you, my dear? Most
> certainly. Train service.

> EDIE
> For me. Train service.

> STOREKEEPER
> That's right.

> EDIE
> To where?

> WILL
> Yeah, Storekeeper. Just where
> does this *eight o'clock* train
> go?

> STOREKEEPER
> Where does it go?

He grows thoughtful, introspective. When he
speaks again, it is as if to himself.

STOREKEEPER (CONT'D)
Where does it go... it goes
wherever we want it to go.
Wherever we need it to go.
Wherever we take it, that is
where it will take us. It goes
to grand new worlds, to
fantastical lands, to wondrous
sights and sounds and
dreams.

WILL
(accusing)
You don't know. Do you? It's
the one thing --the only thing-
- that you don't know.

STOREKEEPER
(shrugs)
No one knows where the train
goes. How can we? Not until
we get there.

EDIE
And I'm going? On the train?

STOREKEEPER
I'd say that's a safe bet, Edie.
I can't say with absolute
certainty, but it's a fairly safe
bet.
(looks to Will)
And I'm figuring you, as well.
Most likely, most likely.

Storekeeper steps over to the screen door,
opens it to the accompanying sound of
screeching hinges.

STOREKEEPER (CONT'D)
How about we go inside?
Maybe have a bite to eat?

                              WILL
                    Sure. Why not. I can't say as I
                    remember when I ate last.

The LIGHTS slowly begin to DIM, remains
bright enough to see.

Will holds a hand down to Edie.

Edie takes the offered hand and then takes
the steps up onto the porch.

Will allows Edie to go inside first. She passes
by the Storekeeper, who gives her a welcoming
nod.

Storekeeper gives another long look around at
the scene before them.

He smiles pleasantly, gives another slow, easy
nod, then follows Will and Edie inside.

                         LIGHTS continue to DIM.

                         CURTAIN LOWERS.

                                        END OF ACT:

ACT 2

SCENE 1.

AT RISE: The interior of the general store.

Storekeeper stands behind the small lunch counter, arms resting on the counter-top, his focus on the others in his store.

Wayne Saunders sits on one of the two stools at the lunch counter, opposite the Storekeeper. He faces the interior of the store with elbows resting on the counter behind him.

Mrs. Mayfield sits at one of the two tables, her purse in her lap. Peter and Helen Harris sit at the table with her.

Will Dawson, Molly Chandler and Edie Paulsen sit at the other table.

Everyone has either a soda pop or a coffee cup near to hand. A few have whatever is left of the sandwiches they had been eating.

Wayne looks keenly at Edie.

> WAYNE
> Say Edie. It is Edie, right? I
> know you, don't I?

Edie doesn't look at him. She lifts a pop bottle to her lips, takes a drink, sets the bottle back onto the table.

> EDIE
> I don't think so.

                    WAYNE
            Sure I do. Yeah, I'm just
            about positive. I've seen you
            somewhere.

He thinks on it a moment. Then another
moment.

                    WAYNE (CONT'D)
            Chicago. Yeah, yeah. You
            been to Chicago?

Edie now does glance up at Wayne, then looks
casually over at   Will and Molly, who are
sitting at the table with her. She looks down
at her soda.

                    EDIE
            Sorry, Wayne. I don't think
            I've heard of it.

                    WAYNE
                (chuckles)
            Yeah, right.

Molly furrows her brow.

                    MOLLY
            Chicago... it's back east,
            right?

                    WAYNE
            What? No. You guys are
            messin' with me, right?
            Chicago... Windy City? Chi-
            Town? Heart of America? The
            Big Onion?

He quotes from the song then, almost but not
quite singing:

>   WAYNE (CONT'D)
> "My Kind of Town - Chicago
> Is"?

Most of those in the room wear blank stares,
but not the Storekeeper.

>   STOREKEEPER
> Of course, Wayne. Chicago.

>   MRS. MAYFIELD
>   (soothing)
> Yes, Mr. Saunders. Chicago. A
> wonderful city.

>   WAYNE
> Right.

Will believes he knows of the city...

>   WILL
> Yeah. Yeah, Al Capone. A
> gangster.

>   MOLLY
> Really?

>   WILL
> I think so.

>   WAYNE
>   (flustered)
> What's the matter with you
> people?

>   MRS. MAYFIELD
> It has been a long day, Mr.
> Saunders.

WILL
Oh, haven't you heard, Mrs.
Mayfield? It's only eight
o'clock in the morning.

MRS. MAYFIELD
Yes. That's right. I'm so sorry.
My mistake.

STOREKEEPER
Okay, now you're gettin' it.

PETER
Did I miss something?

WILL
Probably. I know I have.

Wayne doggedly shakes his head, turns about
on the stool and leans forward onto the lunch
counter, facing the   Storekeeper.

WAYNE
(surrendering tone)
I give up.

Storekeeper remains ever upbeat.

STOREKEEPER
Don't be so downhearted,
Wayne. It's not so bad. Trust
me.

WAYNE
Why?

STOREKEEPER
Oh, Mr. Saunders, you are a
gloomy Gus, aren't you?

He looks past Wayne to those sitting at the
two tables.

STOREKEEPER (CONT'D)
Did everyone get their fill?

Mrs. Mayfield holds up the last small piece of her sandwich.

MRS. MAYFIELD
Why, yes. Thank you very
much. I hadn't realized just
how famished I was.

She sets the bit of sandwich down onto the open paper napkin spread on the table in front of her, brushes her hands together to wipe away any remaining crumbs, and looks across the table at Peter and Helen Harris.

MRS. MAYFIELD (CONT'D)
It was quite tasty. Don't you
think?

HELEN
Yes it was, Mrs. Mayfield. It
was very good.

PETER
Yes. Very good.
(beat)
Say, Mrs. Mayfield. Have you
been on the road long?
Traveling, I mean?

Mrs. Mayfield repeats her earlier statement verbatim, in an almost mechanical, oft-repeated tone.

MRS. MAYFIELD
Cecilia asked if I might stay
with her for a spell. She's all
alone, now that her husband
Walter passed away.

                    PETER
          I see...
               (beat)
          That's where you're headed,
          then? To Cecilia's?

                    MRS. MAYFIELD
          Yes. Cecilia. My sister. She
          asked if I might stay with her
          for a spell.

                    PETER
          Right...
               (increasingly uncomfortable)
          Where does your sister live?

                    MRS. MAYFIELD
          Cecilia? My sister?

Mrs. Mayfield nervously begins straightening
and restraightening the napkin spread out in
front of her.

                    MRS. MAYFIELD (CONT'D)
          I... um...

She delicately pushes aside the napkin and
the remaining bit of sandwich. She brings her
black, plastic purse up from her lap,
meticulously places it on the table in front of
her and clutches it protectively.

                    MRS. MAYFIELD (CONT'D)
          Oh, dear. I must apologize.
          Isn't this something? I'm
          afraid it's gone completely out
          of my head for the moment.
          Flew away. Just like that. I'm
          so sorry.

                    HELEN
That's all right, Mrs. Mayfield.
It's not important. Really.
         (conversational)
So, where are you from, then?

                    MRS. MAYFIELD
         (quickly, confidently)
The south. I'm from the
south.

                    HELEN
         (awkward)
Is that right? The south, you
say?

                    MRS. MAYFIELD
That's right.

She lifts her purse from the table and places it
back down onto her lap.

                    MRS. MAYFIELD (CONT'D)
Yes. I'm from the south.

                    HELEN
         (nervous smile)
That's nice. That's... that's
really, really nice.
         (to Peter)
Isn't it nice, Peter?

                    PETER
Yeah, sure.

Mrs. Mayfield nods curtly and gives Peter and
Helen a wink, sets her jaw and smiles thinly.
A final sharp nod, and then... the conversation
is concluded.

Peter rests a comforting hand on Helen's arm

PETER (CONT'D)
How about we take a breath
of air?

HELEN
Yes. I think that would be...
just splendid.
(looks to Mrs. Mayfield)
Would you excuse us, Mrs.
Mayfield?

Mrs. Mayfield gives a dismissive nod.

END OF SCENE SEQUENCE:

As Peter and Helen stand, the LIGHTS slowly
DIM, though it remains bright enough to see.

Helen and Peter walk to the door leading out
to the front porch, continue offstage.

Wayne spins slowly around on his stool. He
stands and heads to the back of the store,
past the "restrooms" sign, continues offstage.

Will Dawson stands then. He picks his coffee
cup up from the table and walks casually to
the lunch counter. He sets the cup down and
slides it toward Storekeeper as he leans
against the counter.

As the LIGHT continues to DIM, Storekeeper
reaches below the counter and brings up a
coffee carafe. He fills Will's cup, returns the
carafe beneath the counter.

END OF SCENE:

SCENE 2.

LIGHTS slowly return to normal.

Mrs. Mayfield sits alone at one table. Molly Chandler and Edie Paulsen sit at the other table.

Will Dawson stands leaning against the lunch counter, opposite the Storekeeper, behind the counter.

Will straightens and starts back to the table with his coffee. There comes the haunting SOUND of a TRAIN WHISTLE in the distance.

Will stops and turns back to Storekeeper.

> WILL
> So, Storekeeper. It's eight
> o'clock, then?

> STOREKEEPER
> That's right, Will.

> WILL
> (matter-of-factly)
> And yet... it's always eight
> o'clock.

> STOREKEEPER
> Right.

> WILL
> (observation more than a
> question)
> And you don't find anything
> odd about that...

> STOREKEEPER
> Not at all. It's eight o'clock.
> Therefore, it is eight o'clock.

Will gives a nod of the head and takes a sip of his coffee.

> WILL
> Odd universe ya got here,
> Storekeeper.

> STOREKEEPER
> I take that as a compliment.

Will turns back toward the table.

> WILL
> That... is not a surprise.

He indicates the "To Trains" sign hanging on the back wall beside a hallway. It looks exactly the same as the sign outside.

> WILL (CONT'D)
> And you say there's a train
> station behind your store...
> it's through there?

> STOREKEEPER
> It's not far. Quite a lovely
> little place.

Will pulls out his chair and takes his seat.

> WILL
> I don't recall seeing it.

> STOREKEEPER
> No need to see it just yet. But
> soon. We'll have to head over
> there soon.

                    MOLLY
            We're taking a train?

Edie picks up her pop, holds the bottle up in
salute.

                    EDIE
            So the man says.

She takes a drink, sets the bottle back on the
table.

                    EDIE (CONT'D)
                (to Molly)
            Did you have plans to take a
            train ride today? I know that I
            didn't have plans to take the
            train today. Not that I can
            remember.
                (beat)
            But then, I really don't
            remember much of anything.

                    MOLLY
            Train? Train? No. No, I didn't.
                (anxious)
            I don't have much money.
                (repeats to the Storekeeper)
            I don't have much money.

                    STOREKEEPER
            Not to worry, sweetheart.
            Train fare is on the house.

                    MOLLY
            Thank you. That's very nice of
            you.
                (beat)
            Where are we going?

Will snickers lightly at that, recalling the
answer he got when he had asked that same
question earlier.

> WILL
> Yes, Storekeeper. Please, do
> tell the young lady where we
> are going.

Storekeeper smiles warmly, not offended in
the slightest at Will's light jab.

> STOREKEEPER
> We'll know when we get
> there, Molly.
> (sharp nod of the head)
> We will surely know when we
> get there.

Mrs. Mayfield perks up a might, grasps tightly
at her purse.

> MRS. MAYFIELD
> I was on a train once. With
> my dear Herbert.
> (nostalgic smile)
> Oh, so many years ago. We
> took the train to... oh, dear,
> I'm not sure now just where.
> It was a pleasant trip. Yes.
> Though it was an <u>awfully</u> hot
> day. I do remember that. And
> the bologna sandwiches we
> brought along with us? They
> were very warm. You know
> how bologna sandwiches can
> get.

Mrs. Mayfield retreats back into her thoughts,
and the others grow politely silent.

The silence is broken only when Peter and
Helen come back through the door and
onstage.

Peter has a cell phone in hand. He speaks to
no one in particular as they continue to the
table at which Mrs. Mayfield quietly sits.

> PETER
> (indicating his cell phone)
> No signal. I mean, nothing at
> all.

> STOREKEEPER
> Oh, no, no, no, Peter. You
> won't be able to use that
> here. Oh, my no.

Molly looks curiously at the strange object in
Peter's hand as Peter and Helen reach the
other table.

> MOLLY
> What is that?

> PETER
> (absently)
> My phone.

> MOLLY
> Your what?

Peter and Helen both sit down. Peter looks
over at Molly at the other table. He holds up
his phone.

> PETER
> My phone. Ya' know... phone?

> MOLLY
> Really? Your own telephone?

                    PETER
          Uh, yeah...

                    MOLLY
          Can I see it? Do ya' mind?

Peter hands her his phone.

                    PETER
          Yeah. Sure. No problem. It's
          just a lousy phone. Nothing
          fancy.
               (turns back to his table)
          And apparently totally useless
          here.

Molly admires the phone without fully
comprehending what it is that she's holding.

Peter looks to Storekeeper.

                    PETER (CONT'D)
          Do you have a land line I can
          use?

                    STOREKEEPER
          I'm sorry, Peter. There really
          isn't much use for one here.

                    PETER
          I don't know about that. I
          could use one now.

                    STOREKEEPER
          And just who would you call,
          my friend?

PETER
Well, I was going to call--
(suddenly uncertain,
confused)
I, uh... well, I was...
(looks to Helen)
Help me out here, Helen. Who
was I going to call?

HELEN
I don't know. I don't
remember.

PETER
Hmm. Funny. A minute ago I
was all fired up to call
somebody. For the life of me,
I can't remember who.

Molly hands the cell phone back to Peter.

MOLLY
How does it work?

Peter stuffs the phone back into his pocket.

PETER
Didn't you hear? It doesn't.

Wayne returns onstage from the back of the
store. He walks toward the lunch counter.

WAYNE
What doesn't?

MOLLY
His own personal telephone.

WAYNE
(loses interest fast)
Yeah?

WAYNE (CONT'D)
(slides onto the stool)
Ain't that just a real shocker.

MOLLY
It's probably cuz it's not
connected up to anything.

WAYNE
(laughs lightly)
Yeah, no doubt.
(looks to Storekeeper)
So what's the plan, Stan?
What's the way, Ray?

STOREKEEPER
The plan?
(beat)
Well, such as there is a plan, I
suppose it would be simply
that we will all soon walk over
to the station in anticipation
of the train's arrival.

WAYNE
Good plan. Good plan.
(beat)
Somebody going on a trip?

MOLLY
We all are.

WAYNE
Is that so?

STOREKEEPER
(kind smile)
We can only hope.

EDIE
What's that supposed to
mean? Are we going to the
train station or not?

> STOREKEEPER
> Oh my, yes. We are all going
> to the station, Edie. That is
> why you are here. That's why
> you have all come to my
> store... to the center of the
> universe.

> EDIE
> If that's so, then what do you
> mean that we can only hope?

> STOREKEEPER
> Excuse me?

> EDIE
> You said a moment ago... we
> can only hope we are all
> going.

Storekeeper continues his increasingly annoying *knowing* manner as he provides his easy yet thoughtful response.

> STOREKEEPER
> Ah. Yes. We draw nearer that
> moment in the great narrative
> where the determination will
> be made. The epochal
> decision that awaits each one
> of us. Each one of you.
> (beat)
> We shall all go to the train
> station. We shall all be there
> when the train arrives at the
> gate. Of that, I am certain. I
> have no doubt. But as to who
> is to board that train? That I
> cannot say.

> MOLLY
> Why not?

                    STOREKEEPER
          Because I don't know, dear
          girl. The decision has not yet
          been made.

                    WAYNE
          What the heck are you talkin'
          about, Storekeeper?

The Storekeeper takes a long, thoughtful
pause, and when he speaks again, it is with
considerable patience.

                    STOREKEEPER
          You have always known all
          that you needed to know in
          order to take each next step
          in the story that has been
          your life. Have you not?

                    WAYNE
          Well, I --

                    STOREKEEPER
          Oh, you may have had
          doubts, concerns, questions,
          but in the end you were able
          to take that step. At each and
          every critical moment.

                    WAYNE
               (uncertain)
          I suppose.

Storekeeper grows more somber. His tone is
suddenly more serious than it has ever been.

          STOREKEEPER
That is the way of it, Wayne.
And always has been. For
you...
     (to the group at large)
For all of you. You are truly
unique.
     (beat)
The next step will come when
it will come. For each of us. It
most certainly will.

Again the SOUND of the TRAIN WHISTLE in
the distance. Storekeeper lifts his gaze
upward.

The train passes and the sound slowly fades.

          STOREKEEPER (CONT'D)
Let us make our way to the
station, my friends.

Wayne turns about and slides off the lunch
counter stool.

          WAYNE
Heck. Might as well. Nothin'
much keepin' us here.

Wayne approaches the tables. He stops behind
Edie and holds the chair as she slides back
and stands.

          WAYNE (CONT'D)
Miss Paulsen.

          EDIE
Thank you.

They walk toward the hallway opening beside which hangs the "To Trains" sign, continue offstage.

Storekeeper steps around the lunch counter and approaches the tables.

                    STOREKEEPER
          Folks?

                    WILL
          Oh, I s'pose so.
               (to Molly)
          Molly? Shall we?

They stand and step away from their table, follow Wayne and Edie offstage.

Storekeeper steps up to the table with Peter, Helen and Mrs. Mayfield.

                    STOREKEEPER
          And how about you folks? You
          all ready to head over to the
          station?

Mrs. Mayfield appears quite calm. She does not yet stand.

Peter and Helen look anxious, even a bit afraid.

                    HELEN
          The train? Do you really think
          this is necessary?

                    STOREKEEPER
          Absolutely, Helen. It is, after
          all, the reason you are here.

> PETER
> How can you know that? How
> can you know for sure that's
> why we're here?

> STOREKEEPER
> There can be no other reason.
> You are here, you have come
> here, you will go now to the
> station, because you are...
> you. Each of you... you are...
> *you.*

Helen looks anxiously across at Peter.

Peter reaches out and takes her hand.

> PETER
> We might as well.

He waits for Helen to come to terms with it.
Helen finally takes a long breath and nods.

> HELEN
> Okay. Let's go.

> STOREKEEPER
> Good. Good. Very good.

Helen and Peter stand.

Storekeeper focuses attention now on Mrs.
Mayfield.

She remains seated, clutching at the plastic
purse in her lap. She watches Peter and Helen
leave the stage.

Storekeeper pulls one of the now-empty chairs
to him and sits down facing Mrs. Mayfield.

STOREKEEPER (CONT'D)
Mrs. Mayfield? How are you
doing?

MRS. MAYFIELD
I'm doing just fine, sir. How
'bout yourself?

STOREKEEPER
I couldn't be better.
(beat)
Are you ready to join the
others?

MRS. MAYFIELD
Oh, I don't know. I was
thinking I might just stay
here. I mean, after all, I
haven't even finished my
coffee and sandwich.

STOREKEEPER
Mrs. Mayfield, I couldn't let
you do that.

MRS. MAYFIELD
(smile)
Oh, you go on ahead. I'll be
fine. I promise not to pilfer
anything.

STOREKEEPER
Mrs. Mayfield.

Mrs. Mayfield's expression turns knowing, as
does her tone of voice.

MRS. MAYFIELD
I don't imagine it'll take long.
When the time comes. Do
you?

STOREKEEPER
No. No, I'm sure it won't.

MRS. MAYFIELD
Well then, I'll just sit right
here until it's over.

STOREKEEPER
No, ma'am. I really can't let
you do that.
(determined)
Your presence is required at
the train station.

MRS. MAYFIELD
Sir?

STOREKEEPER
You will be on that train when
it leaves.

MRS. MAYFIELD
D'you really think so?

STOREKEEPER
Oh yes. I do. I most certainly
do.

He stands then, holds out a hand for Mrs.
Mayfield to grasp.

The LIGHTS begin to DIM, though it remains
bright enough to see.

Mrs. Mayfield looks up into Storekeeper's face,
smiles warmly and takes his hand.

She stands. Storekeeper supports her as the
two walk toward the opening beside the "To
Trains" sign.

The LIGHTS continue to DIM as they continue
across the stage.

The CURTAIN LOWERS.

END OF ACT:

ACT 3

SCENE 1.

AT RISE: The interior of the train station.

The Storekeeper stands behind the ticket window. He now wears a black suit coat and a cap on his head.

Mrs. Mayfield sits at one end of the bench, her purse in her lap. Edie and Molly are sitting together at the other end.

Peter and Helen are beyond the gate opening, visible through the opening, standing with their backs to the stage. They are watching for the train.

Will steps into view at the gate opening, enters onstage. He steps up to the ticket window and rests an elbow on the counter. From here he can talk with those on the bench in the middle of the station and to Storekeeper.

>   WILL
> Wayne is out there putting
> pennies on the track.

>   MOLLY
> How is he going to collect
> them if he's going with us?

>   WILL
> That's what I asked him.
>   (shrugs)
> He said he'd have time.

Edie turns to the Storekeeper with the hint of
a smirk on her face.

                    EDIE
          What do you say to that,
          Storekeeper? Will he have
          enough time? Maybe all the
          time in the world?

                  STOREKEEPER
          If you mean is he going to be
          on the train when it leaves, I
          couldn't say. Not for certain.
          Not just yet.

                    EDIE
          Not just yet? Well, that's
          downright intriguing. You
          don't know yet, but you will?
          Are you saying that you <u>will</u>
          know? That you'll know who is
          going and who isn't?

                  STOREKEEPER
             (finger to the brim of his hat)
          I wear the hat of the ticket
          agent now, Miss Paulsen. The
          ticket agent usually knows
          who's getting on the train...
             (tip of the hat)
          ... and who isn't.

                    EDIE
             (smile)
          More mysterious yet...

                    MOLLY
             (increasingly anxious)
          But... shouldn't we all go?
          Shouldn't we all get on the
          train?

Edie continues to look at Storekeeper as she
answers Molly.

> EDIE
> I guess that's not really up to
> us, Molly. The decision is out
> of our hands.
> (directly to Storekeeper)
> That right, Storekeeper?

> STOREKEEPER
> That's right.

> EDIE
> But it's not in <u>your</u> hands,
> either. Is it?

> STOREKEEPER
> No, ma'am. It certainly is not.

> EDIE
> And you don't know where the
> train is going.

> STOREKEEPER
> Won't know that until it gets
> there.

> EDIE
> Yes. So you said.

> STOREKEEPER
> Yes, ma'am.

> MOLLY
> I don't want to be left behind.

She scoots forward and stands up. She looks
at Storekeeper.

MOLLY (CONT'D)
I don't want to be left behind.

Edie leans forward on the bench, reaches out and places a hand gently on Molly's arm.

EDIE
It's all right, sweetie. I'm sure you'll be going.

MOLLY
(looks back at Edie)
You don't know that.
(back to Storekeeper)
You don't know that.

STOREKEEPER
No I don't.

MRS. MAYFIELD
Don't you worry, dear. Comes to that, I'll stay here with you.

STOREKEEPER
That's very thoughtful of you, Mrs. Mayfield. But you know very well that's not how it works.

This comment makes just about everyone mighty curious.

WILL
Is that right, Mrs. Mayfield? You know how this works?

                    MRS. MAYFIELD
          Odd, really. But I think so.
          Not that I could put any of it
          into words, mind you, but
          there's things spinnin' round
          in my head. Bits o' knowledge
          and curiosities, and I've no
          idea how any of it got there.
          But it's all there just the
          same.
               (sigh)
          I just can't seem to wrap my
          head 'round any of it. Seems,
          more I focus, the more it slips
          away.

                    WILL
          I'm really sorry to hear that.
               (to Storekeeper)
          I'll bet you could, though,
          couldn't you? Ya' got your
          mind wrapped around it?

The Storekeeper considers the question for a
moment, answers with sincerity.

                    STOREKEEPER
               (thoughtful)
          What I need to know comes to
          me when I need to know it. I
          cannot reach out for it. It
          must come to me.

                    MRS. MAYFIELD
               (distant)
          It's like shadows in a mist. If
          you try to make out the
          shapes, they fade to gray.

                    STOREKEEPER
          Just so, Mrs. Mayfield. Just so.

MOLLY
I'm gonna go outside.

She starts toward the gate. Edie stands up
and follows after her.

EDIE
I'll go with you, Molly. I seem
to recall that I enjoy standing
at the tracks, watching for the
train. Although... I don't ever
remember ever actually doing
that.

The two of them step through the gate and
disappear offstage.

Peter and Helen, still visible beyond the
opening, follow them and also disappear from
view.

WILL
Well, Storekeeper, Mr. Ticket
Agent... you appear to be
frightening off the clientele.

STOREKEEPER
Not to worry, Will. All shall be
right enough before the train
gets here.

He glances to his right. He sees something on
the counter that wasn't there before.

STOREKEEPER (CONT'D)
Ah! Here we go. So it begins
in earnest.

He picks up a brochure-sized piece of paper.
It's a TRAIN TICKET. He takes an envelope
sleeve from a stack on the counter and slips
the ticket into the sleeve.

                    WILL
              (wary)
          Waddya have there,
          Storekeeper?

Storekeeper ignores the question, steps from
behind the counter, holds up the ticket
envelope as he approaches Mrs. Mayfield.

                 STOREKEEPER
          Madam, I have your ticket.

                 MRS. MAYFIELD
          Oh, my. Do you really?

Storekeeper takes up position in front of Mrs.
Mayfield. He gives a half-bow as he hands her
the ticket.

                 STOREKEEPER
          Here you are, Mrs. Mayfield.

                 MRS. MAYFIELD
          Oh dear.
              (clutches the ticket and her
              purse)
          Oh dear. Thank you, sir.

                 STOREKEEPER
              (half bow)
          You are very welcome. You
          enjoy your journey.

                 MRS. MAYFIELD
          I most certainly shall.

Will speaks to Storekeeper as the other
returns to his place behind the ticket counter.

                              WILL
                         (hint of annoyance)
                    Is that how this is going to
                    go? We'll find out who's taking
                    the train one at a time,
                    whenever you feel like
                    handing out a ticket?

                         STOREKEEPER
                    I will distribute the tickets as
                    they come to me.

                              WILL
                    Come to you? You mean--

                         STOREKEEPER
                    As they come to me.

                              WILL
                    You really tellin' me you don't
                    have the tickets back there
                    waiting to be handed out?

                         STOREKEEPER
                    As tickets are made available,
                    I will present them to those
                    named on the ticket.

Will gives the Storekeeper a long, thoughtful
study.

                              WILL
                    You are the odd one,
                    Storekeeper.

                         STOREKEEPER
                    Yes. I suppose that is so.
                         (grin)
                    But then, as you have already
                    observed, I live in an odd
                    universe.

At that moment, Wayne appears in the gate
opening and comes into the station.

> WAYNE
> You most certainly do.

He approaches the end of the counter, leans
an elbow on the countertop.

> WAYNE (CONT'D)
> I've been talkin' with that kid.
> What's her name? Molly? Ya'
> know she's never seen a
> television? She's never even
> heard of 'em.

> WILL
> That's kinda' odd. I know a lot
> a' motel rooms got 'em
> nowadays. You'd a thought
> she would of run across one--

> WAYNE
> (cuts him off)
> What? That's not the--
> (what the heck's going on
> here?)

> STOREKEEPER
> (patiently)
> It's not really all that
> surprising, Wayne. We each
> walk through our own
> individual worlds, live our
> lives through individual
> experiences.

                    WAYNE
You can paint it with all the
philosophizing you want,
Storekeeper. She should know
from televisions. And now I
think on it, she looked at that
couple's cell phone like it was
magic.

                    WILL
Yes. I was wondering about
that, myself.

Wayne gives Will a questioning look.

                    WAYNE
Say... buddy...
        (beat)
 I'm gettin' an idea here.
        (beat)
Tell me... what year is it?

                    WILL
        (confused)
Year?

                    WAYNE
Year. A simple question. What
year is it?

                    WILL
I uh...

                    WAYNE
Uh, huh. You tellin' me you
don't know what year it is?
        (to Storekeeper)
Okay, so you tell me how he
doesn't know what year it is.

                STOREKEEPER
Will doesn't know what year it
is because the year has never
been an issue for him.

                WAYNE
What?

                WILL
     (anxious)
Storekeeper... I told you. I
told you...
     (soft, lost)
I have... *holes*... in my mind.
I should know what year it is.
I told you... there's stuff I
should know that I don't
know.

                STOREKEEPER
My friend, in all the story that
has been your life, what
importance the year? Has the
subject ever come up? It has
not. What matter does it have
now?

                WILL
But...
     (slowly shakes his head)
No. Don't start twisting this
around like it doesn't matter.
It *should* have come up. It
should have come up.
     (leans against the counter)
Sometime. It should have
come up. Shouldn't it? At
some point, some time?
Sometime in my life?

> WAYNE
> Of course it should have.
> What kinda' crazy talk is this?

Wayne pushes away from the counter,
saunters over to the long bench and plops
himself down. He slaps his palms together.

> WAYNE (CONT'D)
> Okay. Okay... Think this
> through. We gotta be on
> drugs or somethin'.

He points to the Storekeeper.

> WAYNE (CONT'D)
> That guy is messing with our
> minds big time.
> (beat)
> It's some kinda' experiment.
> (to Storekeeper)
> You a scientist or a doctor or
> something?

> STOREKEEPER
> No. No, I'm just a
> storekeeper.
> (indicates their
> surroundings)
> And, on occasion, a ticket
> agent, it would seem.

The Storekeeper glances to his right for a
second time. Another ticket sits on the
counter. He reaches over and picks it up.

> STOREKEEPER (CONT'D)
> Ah. And here we go. Mr.
> Dawson. Your ticket, sir.

Storekeeper slips the ticket into a sleeve. He
hands the ticket across the counter.

Will takes the ticket, looks at it, only half comprehending.

> WILL
> (mumble)
> Thank you.

> MRS. MAYFIELD
> Well isn't that nice.

> WILL
> I'm going then.

> STOREKEEPER
> Yes, sir. It looks that way.

> WAYNE
> (to Will, hint of smirk)
> Did you ever doubt it?

> WILL
> Actually, yes.

> WAYNE
> I didn't. You always struck me
> as one of the surviving
> characters.

> WILL
> I'm afraid I don't understand.

Wayne leans back, rests his arms on the back of the bench.

> WAYNE
> The way I'm seein' it, some of
> us are gonna survive this
> thing, some of us aren't. You
> are one of the survivors. I saw
> that right from the start.

>   STOREKEEPER
> Mr. Saunders, a lot of
> protagonists don't live
> through their own stories.

>   WAYNE
> That may be, but we're all
> protagonists here, aren't we,
> Storekeeper?

The Storekeeper appears taken aback at
Wayne's observation.

>   STOREKEEPER
> That's very perceptive, Mr.
> Saunders. I believe you are...
> almost... correct.

>   WAYNE
>   (grin)
> Almost, huh?

>   STOREKEEPER
> I believe so.

>   WAYNE
> Yeah, well, we may not all be
> the hero, but we each come
> from our very own story.

>   STOREKEEPER
> Ah, yes...
>   (beat)
> Isn't that always the case,
> Wayne?

Wayne brings his arms down, leans forward.

WAYNE
You're not gonna get by using
your slippery words this time,
Storekeeper. I'm startin' to
get a handle on this thing,
and you know it.

END OF SCENE SEQUENCE:

The LIGHTS begin to DIM, though it remains
bright enough to see.

Will steps away from the counter. He
approaches Mrs. Mayfield.

WILL
Shall we, Mrs. Mayfield?

Will assists Mrs. Mayfield to her feet and the
two of them exit the stage through the gate
just as Helen and Peter enter the station.

The Storekeeper places two tickets into sleeves
and brings them out to Peter and Helen.

Peter and Helen sit down on the bench beside
Wayne.

Peter pats Helen's hand. They sit quietly
clinging to their tickets.

The LIGHTS continue to DIM.

END OF SCENE:

SCENE 2.

LIGHTS slowly return to normal.

The Storekeeper puts together another ticket
packet, slips a ticket into a sleeve.

He smiles as Edie comes through the gate and
into the station.

          STOREKEEPER
Ah, Miss Paulsen. I have your
ticket.

          EDIE
Thank you. I must admit, this
is a relief.
      (to counter, collects ticket)
Though for the life of me, I
couldn't tell you why.

          WAYNE
Probably because it _is_ for the
life of you.

          EDIE
What would make you say
such a thing?

          WAYNE
Really? Tell me, what do you
think is going to happen to
anyone left behind? Might this
poor lost soul simply walk out
of here? To where?

          EDIE
I couldn't say.

                    WAYNE
          Let's make it a little more
          personal. If you hadn't been
          given a ticket, where would
          you go once the train pulled
          out of the station, leaving you
          standing out there on the
          platform waving bye-bye?

                    EDIE
          I don't know...

                    STOREKEEPER
          Now, Wayne... no need to
          upset the lady. She has her
          ticket, after all.

Wayne turns his attention to the Storekeeper.

                    WAYNE
          Yes. And that leaves just me
          and the girl now, doesn't it?
               (beat)
          How many you figure are
          going to be stayin' on here
          after the train leaves,
          Storekeeper?

                    STOREKEEPER
          I have no way of knowing.

                    WAYNE
          Is that right?

                    STOREKEEPER
          That is a fact.

                    EDIE
               (looking around the station)
          Um, I have to... uh...

Storekeeper points offstage.

>   STOREKEEPER
>   Of course. Right through
>   there, Miss Paulsen.

>   EDIE
>   Thank you.

Edie quickly leaves.

For the moment, only Wayne and the
Storekeeper are in the station.

Wayne lets his defenses drop, shows
trepidation.

>   WAYNE
>   I'm not going, am I?

>   STOREKEEPER
>   I really don't know. I had
>   been fairly certain that you
>   were, but now... now I don't
>   know.

>   WAYNE
>   What made you so sure?
>   Before?

The Storekeeper stumbles in his thoughts.

>   STOREKEEPER
>   I just thought... you were...
>   *needed*.

>   WAYNE
>   I'm not now. I'm not...
>   needed...

                    STOREKEEPER
          Something has changed. At
          least, I think something has
          changed. Something is
          different.
                    (beat)
          I can feel it.

                    WAYNE
          Yeah.
                    (leans back, hands clasped
                    in his lap)
          Me too.

The Storekeeper looks to one side. Another
train ticket. He picks it up.

                    STOREKEEPER
          Another train ticket.
                    (places it in a sleeve)
          It's Molly's.

                    WAYNE
                    (genuine)
          I'm glad. Good for her.

                    STOREKEEPER
          Yes. Good for her.

                    WAYNE
          I wonder what role she will
          play? Once the train arrives at
          its destination.

                    STOREKEEPER
          Odd you should ask that, in
          just that way. I was
          wondering the very same
          thing.

                    WAYNE
What about you, Storekeeper?
Will you be going? When the
train leaves?

                    STOREKEEPER
No. My own *role*, as you say,
will play itself out here.
        (admiring his station)
My train station. My general
store.
        (long pause)
My world.

                    WAYNE
The center of the universe.

                    STOREKEEPER
We are at its very heart.

The Storekeeper steps from behind the
counter, starts toward the gate.

                    STOREKEEPER (CONT'D)
I think I'll give Molly her
ticket.

He walks through the gate opening, turns
right and disappears from view.

Wayne sits up, leans forward. He stands,
pauses, walks to the ticket counter and leans
over, calmly looks at where the tickets usually
show up.

Edie comes back into the station from the
restroom.

                    EDIE
Where is everyone?

Wayne shrugs, wanders back toward to the
bench.

> WAYNE
> Waitin' for the train, I expect.
> Growing impatient, no doubt.

Edie walks to the gate opening, looks out. She
turns back and looks around the station.

> EDIE
> But not you?

> WAYNE
> I am yet to be blessed with a
> ticket.

He climbs up on the bench, sits on the back,
feet on the seat. He clasps his hands together.

> WAYNE (CONT'D)
> You do remind me of
> someone, you know... but
> you're not her.

> EDIE
> I know.

> WAYNE
> You are her, but you're not.

Edie walks to the bench, sits down at the far
end.

> EDIE
> Friend of yours?

> WAYNE
> Nah. Not really. Just someone
> I knew.

        EDIE
And I'm her, but I'm not her...

        WAYNE
The two of you were written
different. You came later, I
think.

        EDIE
Okay... that's deep. I guess.
Very weird, but probably
deep.

        WAYNE
That's me. Deep all over.
    (beat)
Now, anyway.

        EDIE
    (thoughtful)
I do sense the change.
    (more thoughtful still)
And then there's the
Storekeeper. He knew me,
too.

        WAYNE
The Storekeeper knows
everyone who comes to his
store.

        EDIE
I don't get it. We've never
met. I'm certain of that.
    (taps at her temple)
There's a lot I'm missing in
there, but I would definitely
remember him.

Wayne slides down from the back of the
bench, sits down properly.

                    WAYNE
The Storekeeper knows us
because he knows the books
we come from.

                    EDIE
        (bewildered)
What? Sorry, but that
doesn't make any sense.

                    WAYNE
The woman you reminded me
of? She's a dancer. Pretty
good one. She works at a club
I used to go to when I was
living in Chicago.

                    EDIE
What does that have to do
with me? Or with books?

                    WAYNE
She's a character from the
book I'm from. And you, I'm
guessing you're a rework of
that same character, only in
another book.

                    EDIE
That's crazy. Mr. Saunders,
you have most assuredly lost
it.

                    WAYNE
And Molly... she's from a book
with no televisions. Will
Dawson, he's probably from
fifty, sixty years ago, his
character spent a lot of time
living out of motels while
doing his archeology stuff.

                    WAYNE (CONT'D)
                    (beat)
            We're all from different
            stories... different worlds. We
            know as much as our
            characters needed to know...
            as much as the writer thought
            we needed to know. The
            worlds we know are only as
            complete as our stories
            needed them to be.

Edie twists about uncomfortably and sits up
straight.

                    EDIE
            All right. Let's say this is all
            true. I'm not buying it, you're
            insane, and possibly
            dangerous, but let's say that
            everything you're saying is
            true. So, what are we doing
            here? How did we
            miraculously jump out of
            these mysterious books of
            yours and show up here?

                    WAYNE
            Well, I think... I'm pretty
            sure... that our writer, our...
            creator I guess you'd call him,
            is trying to decide which of his
            characters from earlier books
            are going to be in his next
            one.

He leans in Edie's direction, speaks
conspiratorially.

WAYNE (CONT'D)
Between you and me... I don't
think his books have been all
that successful, but he's not
ready to give up on his
characters.

EDIE
So then, you're saying...
whenever he decides on a
character, a train ticket shows
up.

WAYNE
That's what I'm thinking.

EDIE
And the Storekeeper? Is he...
is he the writer?

WAYNE
I doubt it. No... no, I think...
   (thinks long and hard)
The Storekeeper is like... he's
like... *a librarian*.... he's this
miniature librarian living
inside the writer's head,
keeping track of all his stories
and characters and things like
that.

EDIE
Does he know?

WAYNE
He's starting to figure it out.
Same as me. Heck, even ol'
Mrs. Mayfield is starting to get
it.

                    EDIE
          How did you? Figure it out, I
          mean? Where'd you get all
          this?

                    WAYNE
                   (shrug)
          It's been coming to me in bits
          and pieces. More and more as
          we get closer.

                    EDIE
          Closer to what?

                    WAYNE
          For you? Gettin' on the train,
          taking it to the final
          destination. Taking on your
          'role of a lifetime'.
                   (slowly shakes his head)
          But me? I figure I'm done.

Edie looks as though she may finally accept
all that Wayne has revealed. She believes it.

                    EDIE
          I'm sorry. I really am.

                    WAYNE
          Hey, I was in the running for
          a while.
                   (shrug of shoulder)
          Who knows? Maybe I can
          head back to Chicago. Maybe
          hook up with that dancer.

From a distance comes the haunting SOUND
of the TRAIN WHISTLE.

They both look upward, outward...

                    WAYNE (CONT'D)
          That'd be for you. You better
          go.

                    EDIE
          This isn't right. He can't just...

                    WAYNE
          Just what? Not write me into
          the story?

                    EDIE
          Not now... not now that
          we're...
              (struggles)
          We're here. We're not just
          characters in a book. We're
          not...

She stands then, looks about the station.

                    EDIE (CONT'D)
          We're... *alive*.

                    WAYNE
              (beat)
          I'll be all right. Really. You
          need to get out there.

There is a final, single TRAIN WHISTLE.

                    WAYNE (CONT'D)
          It's here. You go on.

                    EDIE
          Maybe your ticket is here.
          Maybe it came late.

Edie hurries over to the ticket window, leans
over the counter. Nothing...

Wayne stands.

> WAYNE
> Don't worry about me.

He takes her hand, guides her toward the gate opening.

> WAYNE (CONT'D)
> Who knows? Maybe I'll see you in his next book.

> EDIE
> Hey, that's right. You said you were in the running for this one. He must like you.

> WAYNE
> Absolutely. I figure he just didn't have a part for me in this one.

> EDIE
> Yeah. Yeah...

She steps away, has trouble letting go of his hand.

> EDIE (CONT'D)
> I'll see you?

> WAYNE
> Absolutely.

> EDIE
> 'kay.

Edie hesitates, finally turns away. She steps through the gate opening and is gone.

Wayne turns from the gate. He takes a moment to look about at the empty station. He takes several steps back into the station. He stops near the bench.

He rests a hand on the back of the bench, gazes offstage.

The SOUND of the TRAIN WHISTLE. It rises, then slowly fades.

The Storekeeper appears in the gate opening. He steps toward Wayne.

> STOREKEEPER
> You should go collect your
> pennies.

Wayne half turns, speaks without looking at Storekeeper.

> WAYNE
> (questioning)
> Pennies?
> (slow realization)
> Ah. Yes. Pennies. The tracks.
> (beat)
> Maybe later.

The Storekeeper looks warily at Wayne.

> STOREKEEPER
> Wayne?

Wayne puts on a genuinely warm smile.

> WAYNE
> Wayne...
> (shakes his head... no...)
> Wayne is on his way to
> Chicago.

                    STOREKEEPER
                    (realization)
        So you are... *him*...

Wayne takes his time. He looks about then,
indicates their surroundings.

                    WAYNE
        Nice place you have here. And
        I really like your store.

                    STOREKEEPER
        Thank you. It comes from
        your second book.

                    WAYNE
                    (comfortable smile)
        Yes. That's right.

He indicates the station.

                    WAYNE (CONT'D)
                    (nostalgic)
        And this... this comes from
        my very first. I loved that
        book.
                    (starts around the bench)
        I worked on it for almost
        three years.

He sits down. He leans back, admires the
station.

The Storekeeper steps around and sits beside
him.

                    STOREKEEPER
        And... how is the latest book
        coming? I see you have all the
        characters.

LIGHTS slowly begin to DIM, though it
remains bright enough to see.

> WAYNE
> It's coming together real nice,
> Storekeeper. Real nice. Story
> is outlined, characters are
> already getting comfortable.
> Real nice.
> > (beat)
> It's gonna be great. I can feel
> it. This one... this one is going
> to be my masterpiece.

> STOREKEEPER
> That's good. I'm glad.
> > (beat)
> And I'm happy for them.
> They're good people.

Wayne nods, relaxes, continues to admire the
station.

> WAYNE
> We should go over to the
> store later. Get a soda or
> something.
> > (beat, sigh, another easy
> > nod)
> Ah, Storekeeper... I do love
> this place...

LIGHTS continue to DIM.

The CURTAIN LOWERS.

END OF PLAY: